Nijolė Kavaliauskaitė – Hunter

Whispers of music instruments

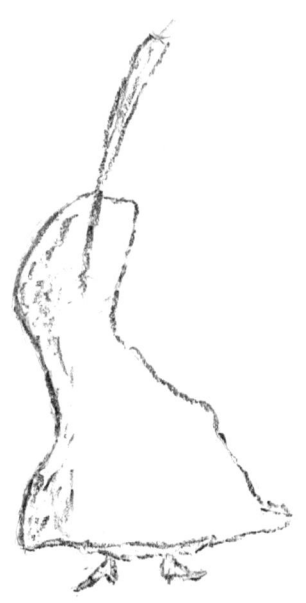

novum ⬠ pocket

© 2025 novum publishing gmbh
Rathausgasse 73, A-7311 Neckenmarkt
office@novum-publishing.co.uk

ISBN 978-3-903468-16-0
Cover photo:
Evellean I Dreamstime.com
Cover design, layout & typesetting:
novum publishing
Internal illustrations:
Nijolė Kavaliauskaitė – Hunter

The images provided by the author have been printed in the highest possible quality.

www.novum-publishing.co.uk

Print product with financial
climate contribution
ClimatePartner.com/16547-2311-1001

Contents

Preface

No way, they're not genderless,' – the author remarked, quoting her Muse, who had imagined the musical instruments as living objects with a soul like a passionate woman or man. The Author got to that conclusion after being obviously astounded by their forms; when she looked at one, she saw that it was shaped like a pear, which gave it a really fruity appearance and of course juicy thoughts which passionately melted in her mouth.

Yummy! – The author shouted and was ready to slice it.

The other one from the instrument collection had a slim, appealing physique, similar to a youthful stupid and hot girlfriend, who preferred to be held between legs and embraced as well. Obviously, her soul would demand from a musician who is also a partner, a precise degree of love, care, and profound commitment. Otherwise, the instrument's soul will refrain from engaging in any action or, if engaged, probably refuse to answer truthfully and goes against the player with all inner resistance.

Mankind invented instruments to engage with as partners in life's game, allowing the performer's soul to feel only joy. When people touch musical instruments, they love to whisper their own secrets, thoughts, and beliefs. After a heartfelt reunion, the reality of being together permeates the air and lingers around the eyes and ears like a pleasant scent. Through their whispering voice, instruments are able to express their dream to the rest of the world. Instruments are unique, they also believe in living a sinless and exemplary life.

A good player cares more about the instrument's soul than how they appear to him. That's why some of them engage like there are truthful partners in bed.

The instruments undoubtedly possess an ideal physique, an ideal outlook, and also have a mysterious spirit that exhibits its own senses. They are full of hope and anticipation to meet someone.

**What is the spirit of
musical instruments whispering?**

Basetlé

Her name is Basetlé. Her outward traits thrill me in a nice way because she is tall and shaped like a beautiful woman. My beau isn't in great demand, and she doesn't want any favours or commitment from me. Basetlé acts as an optimistic romantic girl living in her own world, being bashful and shy and not showing any genuine interest or feeling in me. Only anticipates being held. She is also deafeningly silent, hesitant and unwilling to say anything when it is not asked of her. I'm still waiting for an answer from her which she hesitates to say.

Please, please, please, please, please, please, please, please, please, please, please, please, please. Always, always I need to take appropriate steps as a Possessor to get her to speak with me.

To make her talk, Basetlé must be stuffed between two men's legs and played with her gut-stringed strings. Furthermore, no force is required for this action; all that is required is the desire to develop intimate companionship. Then she wails, depressed from the embrace, at being enslaved, sobbing without hope of emancipation. She trembles as she waits for her Possessor to be entirely fulfilled.

Me as a Possessor clearly admires her for her incredibly slender body, which hasn't changed in years and still looks like an hourglass. Her waist remains slender and tiny, emphasising her broad hips and long, graceful legs. When her Possessor misses her soul, he touches her inner beauty. There is a bow made of horse hairs. In the event of contact with the bow, the instrument's strings are able to reveal how beautiful her soul is.

Her Possessor knows Basetlé differs from the genuinely beloved woman in that she does not make any eye contact. Woman's eyes are windows through which you can peer further into her hidden inner sources, sinking and disintegrating.

Accordion

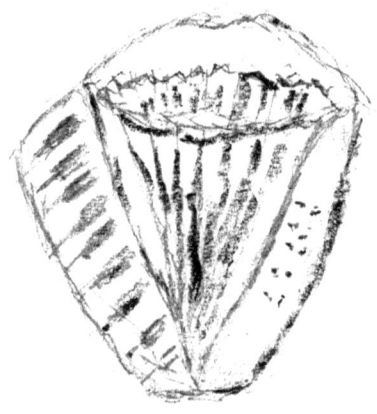

Accordion constantly showing his teeth and curling his lips that may indicate playfulness or excitement. However, his heart is crying, because. he is nothing more than an item that has been customised to meet someone's emotional needs, to fulfil the essence of happiness and well-being.

When the player's heart is in sorrow, and suffers from emotional pain, he pulls the device closer and lovingly hugs the accordion with affection, as if it were his own girlfriend, and experiencing Accordion's passion, his soul escapes into Heaven. The present surrogate senses that there is a lack of consistent warmth between them, and that only inner affection has taken its place.

At the finish line, the player learns that his heart is now empty, and that the peak of oxytocin was released for a reason: to foster short bonding. After a while, Accordion realises that he is no longer attracted to her as a woman, and the connection between the two of them has already been severed. And the former lover waits for the event's eventual outcome. A decision has been reached. The player tosses his passionate girlfriend into a dark corner like a box and goes in search of the true soul.

The Drum

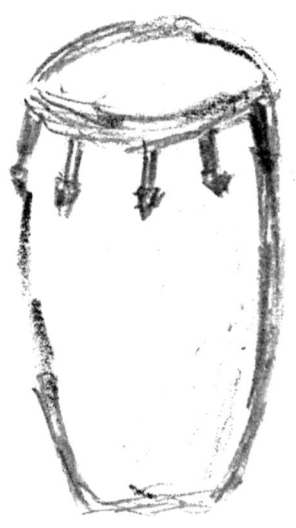

People with an inflated sense of self-worth may assume the Drum is both sluggish and lousy. It is unquestionably the Drums fault for giving the idea that he is difficult to motivate and to achieve anything, that he is only good on a few occasions, one of them unpleasant for his guts. However, by punching himself in the stomach, he is able to dictate the beat to others. Slow starters irritate him, which is why he is so preoccupied with thoughts pushing others. His brain, which is made up of thousands of neurons, does not reflect him properly. Definitely not! One of his distinguishing characteristics is the way he forces others to move. His quirkiness displays his worth, despite his sluggishness. Without Drum, the symphony would be doomed, life would be empty. There would be no movement, and no tomorrow would come.

Horseshoe

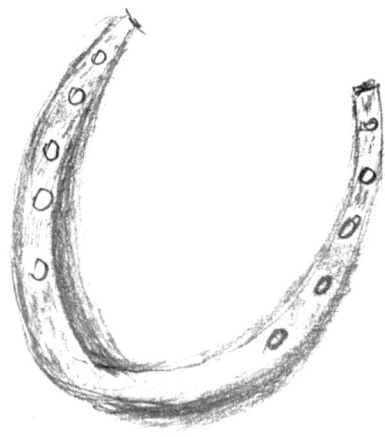

There was more than one artistic Mecca in the world where people tried to play music with horseshoes. The device was modified to create music sounds with the purpose of entertaining people and bringing joy into their lives. Simple minded folks utilised horseshoes for practical purposes, hammering them under the horse's feet to keep it from slipping on the ice. Others, on the other hand, considered the horseshoe to be a source of happiness and pleasure. Throughout the long process of creation, Horseshoe – instrument, as a new product, was formed from a real horseshoe, and given the ability to chirp like a honey bee; therefore, the tongue was added to him. Thought does not steer silently when someone tries to use the horseshoe to please his heart. In order to increase the sound range, it has experimented with other materials such as metal and even wood. Wood to make Horseshoe was chosen for musical reasons because of his fashionable appearance. Tongued Horseshoe, which was made of wood, fits easily. As many people are unaware, Horseshoe is the only one who can remove melancholy from the heart when it is engulfed by sadness and mourning. That's all you'll need to get the Horseshoe out of the pocket. Someone who sees it for the first time has no idea what instrument it is or how intelligent Horseshoe is.

Wind instrument

The Geese's feathers fell out like a woman's broken teeth as she grew older. The woman and the geese both lost their valuables towards the end of their lives in the same way. After a certain amount of time had passed and only one tooth remained, the Geese's loving spirit made the decision to ascend into paradise. No feathers were worn at the location since feathers were no longer valuable; only the innocent soul was. As a non-returnable gift, the bird's last feather was accidentally dropped on the ground where humans trod. The Geese wished for us to rescue it and transform it into a musical instrument that may brighten people's gloomy days.

I felt a warm sensation rush through my entire body when I first saw the feather lying down on the Earth's face, because the savoury and rich taste of her meat had lingered in my stomach since Christmas. There were no other senses left but that of fulfilment after the event. For a while, I had the idea that if I tried holding her feather to make sounds with my lips, I would be able to recapture the souls of those geese. My belief that after-death eternity exists. I was certain that her pure spirit resides therein. Clearly, she heard my pleas and remembered them until a solution was found, so a group of her cousins was assigned to the Earth in the spring. After a short distance, they landed on the lake. Sheep herded by a shepherd moved here on purpose to shield themselves from possible dangerous surroundings.

The lost feather was enthralled by the enthusiasm and took the folks to use for fanfare. When the belly is hungry, the instrument is blown in order to attract and achieve the desired results more effectively.

The French Horn

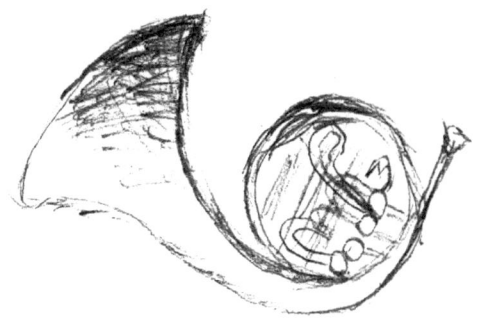

The cherry snail was resting on a grape leaf that had grown up into a slender convolvulus vine with well-shaped leaflets that had attracted everyone's attention. Snail's head was preoccupied with figuring out how to move from here to peace and eternity. She was well aware that life will come to an end at some point. It was something the Snail wishes had happened sooner. There will be no sunsets, no tomorrows, no life, and no unfulfilled dreams.

Meanwhile, the Grape had her own way of looking at and often thinking about life, and her perspective and expectations were different in many ways. As a result, she climbed the window suggestively. She pursued relentlessly to mingle together, bringing them as a unit, dreaming about eternity. But the response from her adorable object wasn't received yet, so she often shook involuntarily. Grape cherished the bright hope of life, Snail planned a sad outcome for herself.

When she looked out the window, she spotted a bright board (TV) with moving boxes from one side to the other. When she glanced closer, she noticed that the soloist was holding her relative in his hands as if she were the entire galaxy. The kin was nurtured. The instrument glittered and released a squeak. She didn't really understand why she did it. Maybe it was because of pleasure. After seeing the action, Snail's face lit up with a joyful, appreciative smile.

She's so beautiful and cheerful!' Snail exclaimed in delight over the view.

The Snail was certain that the pair had a passionate relationship or even unselfish love. Impression was so powerful. Being loved and in love was a major motivator for Snail to continue on with life.

French Horn used to be a Snail that scurried through filthy alleyways in search of her favourite spot on the planet where she could be completely content. She witnessed and understood human life in a way that was inconvenient for her. The ground roared when humans moved, and Snail's heart yearned for something greater. The shell was grown on her in order for her to have a safe and pain-free life. Although the shell's pressure on her body was great, it could ward off problems, and she was attempting to be prudent. She trembles at the sight of them because there are many intercessors on their road, so she flees to hide in the shell, while others defend themselves with their teeth.

She travelled around the world without saying anything to anyone. When he met the serpent, he sought to develop a common language but failed. The Serpent shared its tale of being driven out of paradise in exchange for one word sent into space. He is now remorseful, but nothing can be altered. Time is not a lake full of water; if you're thirsty, drink until you're satisfied; otherwise, everyone would drink it without ever gaining the skills of being wise. The Serpent will have to pay for his misdeeds for the rest of his life by telling everyone his story, in the hopes that the stranger will learn something. After hearing his story, the Snail came to the conclusion that the Earth is the best place for her after hearing tragic evidence. She is not required to fantasise about going somewhere else. After this, her soul and spirit were refreshed. She was ecstatic. As a result, she was able to be reborn as a French horn and enjoy her life to the fullest. She doesn't want the Serpent near her since he's full of wickedness and he might provoke her.

The Violin

The Violin is well aware of her outer beauty and definitely knows her unequalled price. It makes her feel more significant than others. Her body appears to others to be exceptional in terms of its miraculous ability to maintain slim shape.

Her face is more beautiful than anyone else's –, whispered some stupidity loudly.

The Violin appeared to her to be having the best time of her life. The Beauty's voice was divine and unique as well. Even the Nightingale recognizes Violin's talent to sing so passionately. The bird is horrified to learn that, no matter how genuine Nightingale's serenade is, her magnificent voice, which performs spontaneous trills, will not be able to overwhelm Violin's beauty. Nightingale wishes she could be more successful in her career. Recently, the Bird came to the conclusion that she and Violin would not be doing any duet. She is not good enough.

Aside from her inherent talent, the Violin had mastered the art of flirting, and her smooth and sweet voice captivates listeners. Many strangers remained silent after hearing her numerous vibrations. Because the Violin wishes to be praised and blessed for the rest of her life, she is doing music. She is immortal, yet the life of a bird is finite.

Wooden bells

The Wooden Bells were physically worn out by being banged by wooden sticks. After this constant motion, wood realised there is no love between them, and there probably never was. His naive imagination was the only thing that allowed him to make meaningful connections. Bells never dreamed that their once-close friends would turn on them, making them suffer for undetected crimes while they rejoiced. Bell's thoughts drifted, and he realised that a good friend cares about you and enjoys spending time with you. The genuine companion communicates softly and compassionately. This one, on the other hand, has a tremendous desire to touch, which is the most primitive sensation humans have. He is obviously unaware that this kind of touch might cause somebody's heart to grow and shatter into a million pieces. Clearly, the sticks thumping against the wooden bells have no idea that the most beautiful things in the world are not visible or touchable. Peace, Joy, and Love are the notes of the melody of life. Bells, if touched correctly, can boost the spirit, bring peace, and help one to recognize one's own Divinity. Behave in a way that attracts attention.

The Piano

As a gift of his love, God gave the Pianos extraordinarily beautiful teeth. Piano has intended to show off his gorgeous teeth to everyone. He hasn't stopped doing it since then. The Piano's Keyboard, on the other hand, only closed his mouth once when it was in a difficult situation, when the partner in front of him was not fully honest and heartfelt. According to Piano, the Stranger appeared with unintentionally, a tangential interest, inappropriately to touch or maybe exploit. The Keyboard shut his mouth completely then. Other than that, the Keyboard was proud and believed that everyone should see what is hidden in his cavities. By displaying his teeth, he hoped to achieve wholeness, flawlessness, thoroughness, and greatness. Why? It all comes down to his ego, and Piano aspired to achieve perfection in his heart. I'm guessing it has something to do with the ambition to be a celebrity.

Of course, the teeth were grateful and appreciative to God. Piano hasn't forgotten that things like that come from above. Showing his teeth, he also expresses their gratitude to God by making a sound that resembles a morning sunrise, and the novelty of a new day.

One factor, if you know Piano's proper language, it makes you feel more fortunate. Music becomes the nourishment for your spirit.

The Small Drum

Since ancient times, the drum and the dog have been buddies. So, for many years, the skin from the animal's belly was stretched across the hollow drum's large mouth. After this kind of invention, the mouth of the drum was nominated as the most powerful weapon, which was given to make a sound when it needed to run away from an enemy, or to overcome difficult conditions, or to deliver a passionate message to someone by replicating the sender's heartbeats. People believed, if you combine two things like a drum and a dog, you could get a double effect. Meanwhile, the animal's basic emotions, such as joy, fear, and rage, are likely to contribute distinct traits to the drum. It happens when Drum becomes restless and strives for his aim as a result of the dog's indulgence in barking.

When the dog's stomach is empty, his intestines make a gurgling sound, and his stomach growls, as if an orchestra is playing in his head. Things like this irritate the drum, which has borrowed belly from the dog. It harms his psychic and psychological well-being. In order to improve the dog's irritable mood, require a refresher on a materialistic base like meat or at least bones. When the dog's stomach is filled with the food, he becomes deafeningly quiet. So then, the drum develops true peace and harmony.

We like to put food into our stomachs and sip soft drinks in public. But non-materialistic thinking is better for us and for others, thinks the drum.

The Guitar

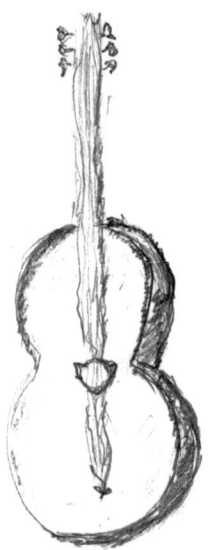

Many people have attempted to look into Guitars inner world in the hopes of finding peace, harmony, and, of course, love. Living a lonely life, the guitar had a hope to find a meaning, purpose, and passion to someone in her life.

The Man was already in there when he asked the Creators, who was also a King of the Universe, the following question:

– What should a woman be?

– Perfect! – in one word said Creator.

– But it's impossible, she's not real? – Man's voice confronted him.

No matter what, the Man continually searched for an answer. The world to him seemed hopeless without the partner. After many days of deep contemplation and observation, he got to the conclusion that the ideal shape only exists in his mind. No matter what, the man kept thinking about the lady of his life. Seeing his contemplation, God decided to help him, sending him a thought to his soul. The Man, receiving some creative energy, worked like an overwhelmed painter, drawing his woman in his dreams. His decision resulted in him bringing something new into his own universe, exerting oneself ferociously for the one and only. The man then used a piece of wood as a construction material. To avoid making it difficult to please her and love her, he chose a thinner, more flexible piece and sat down, focusing on his breathing. He was sure that a woman could bring a sense of balance to his mind, body, and spirit. He started working on her after that. The Man was sure the shape of the woman was her most important feature. To draw attention to her waist, he cautiously carved a tree.

The hips of the sculpted woman had an apparent feminine shape, and they appeared to be two gushing sources on which his arms could rest. The man wasn't born yesterday, and he was well aware that a woman's heart may be deceitful at times. He drilled the hole in order to be able to see her soul in case she tried to deceive him. He could now see how the woman's heart began to pound softly and he was able to understand her thoughts. It was his goal to see her heart. And also, communication was important to him. She should be able to express own feelings of admiration towards him. He added the strings for this purpose, expecting a reciprocal response.

His two hands could hold her body now. In one hand he gripped her long neck, which resembled a beautiful swan. With the second one he touched her strings. He closed his eyes. Since then, they both swam like two birds in his dream lake.

Muddies

Who's to say that mud can't sing?

It doesn't matter that he came from the depths of the Earth. His body had been happily lying there for a long time, and his head had been calmly lying down on Mother Earth's laps, latching her breasts in a magnificent manner. He couldn't be seen with the naked eye, which is why no one knew he was there for so long. The Earth's cohabitant, on the other hand, was not embarrassed or ashamed of its own nature, even if it lived in the dark and was immortal. On the contrary, he was confident that he was in the correct location. The muddy was required to face the Sun in his heart, no matter how happy he was. He was certain that one day, after a lengthy period of hiding, he would appear to say "Hello" to her. He had a distinct shape before it happened, or he didn't have one at all. However, following his encounter with the Sun, the mud decided to transform his ungainly and sticky body into a gleaming one. As a result, the muddy's re-incarnation was motivated to sing the song. Since then, the Mud has been attempting to compete with the birds, even adopting their shape. The birds turn their left and right ears towards the whistling sound after hearing him sing. They had clearly heard the mud's symphony, and they now feel bound by blood. Due to the lack of feathers on muddies, some of the birdies continue to believe they are not birds and don't take them seriously.

The Longwood

The Longwood is located in the middle of the universe, halfway between Heaven and Earth. He obviously lives in the middle of everything. For instance, he is undecided about which career path to take. Whether to strive for a higher level of life, such as that of angels, or to remain trapped in Earth's sin and fight temptation. His wooden nature, on the other hand, whispers to him to stay near the Sauna. He is satisfied with the service which he provides, and has the power to persuade all those on the sides, as well as people of various ideologies, about their hygiene. When the wind blows from the north, Longwood spins his noisy body to the south, enticing men to the Sauna and promising them body rejuvenation, as well as the restoration of youthful vigour and attractiveness. When the wind blows from the east, women are advised to go to the Sauna to shape their bodies in a healthy way.

Longwood is aware of his limitations and that he is un-qualified to master better abilities. As a result of his pro-posal, people are merely assisted in washing dust from their body. Because the Longwood do not know how to care for the Soul, the kin requested that they leave their Soul at the Sauna's entrance. As a result, as a higher self, it may listen to God's vast commandments. Longwood is well aware of his fate and the fact that he is here for the rest of his life.

Bagpipe

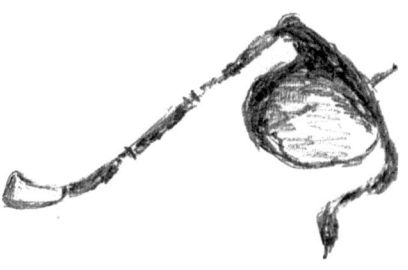

There was a famous Labanora's Forest of Lithuania, which became a well-known location on the planet, with a fortunate small town nearby.

Once upon a time, a foolish Shepherd desired to play the bagpipes so that he might make it a practice to bless God. Because he was preoccupied with an idea, he disobeyed the law and wandered into a nearby wood during the darkest time of the night, which is between twilight and dawn. The Herdsman realised it was the appropriate time for him to achieve his dream. He was able to master two flutes for himself despite the poor visibility and a lack of light. He also realised that if one panpipe breaks, another will step in to fill the void. He put the mastered flutes in a Shepherd's bag, which was fashioned from dried animal's skin, to hide the evidence. He tried to conceal the evidence of his wrongdoing. Flutes were not happy inside since old fashioned and grouchy dried crumbs had sat on the bottom for a long time and did not appear pleasant;

according to them, newcomers were not welcome. The bag was torn as well. Outer look revealed his age.

Meanwhile, the volume of the pipes was too low to bless their Creator, so Shepheard turned to the Lord for help. 'How should I proceed?' said Sheppard. The Lord did not answer, but provided him with some power. The Shepherd, blessed by God, sewed both bagpipes to make it appear as if they were one bladder. And he said, 'Have a lung.' In order to create pleura, he used the skin of a dead cat. Two bagpipes gained one lung in this way. It was simple to play musical pipes; all you had to do was just blow both at the same time. Because of the lung, the pipes could be heard from a long distance. The six holes in one pipe were carved in recognition of the preceding six working days. The seventh day was set apart to bless the Lord. The tune was played on one bagpipe with six holes, while another was used to accompany it. The music made the Shepherd happy and by playing he had the capacity to release and reveal the truth about his life.

The amazing instrument that had been made near Labanora's forest was revealed anonymously by a whistle-blower. It piqued people's attention, causing them to want to learn more about strange events. People from other countries who looked weird, such as a half-man, half-woman – attempted to take the image of a piper and secretly replace it on a piece of paper. They were intrigued by the sight of one extra-terrestrial playing two pipes at the same time, and a strange bladder in his music became active.

Heaven had to come down. The bagpipe of Labanoras turned out to be suitable for the church ceremony and dance.

Dewlap

Dewlap – a piece of jewellery? "Not for me!" – The man thought. - Has no gloss or gold colour. Do not shine when approaching the Sun, do not play with the light. Why do I have to carry it? I will give it to the animal, the one who does not like luxury and does not paint his nails. It works well when tied around an animal's neck. He honestly sheds a tear while enjoying it because it brings him such genuine delight.

Rattle

There aren't many magnificent Man cave masterpieces, like a Rattle, that can not only sound cheerful, but also wake up a soul, leading her through the lies and rising positive feelings above the gloom, boosting appreciation of life. In the past, some people would shake a rattle to ward off an unpleasant ghost who was attempting to harm or terrify an innocent soul to death. With the passing of time, the rattle became accustomed as a toy, used to retain rhythm during a dance, which is a key part of music, or given to a baby to shake to develop motor skills.

Few people are aware that the Rattle of himself is a frightened and careful person who deals with others delicately. The wood is simply her outer shell, designed to attract the human eye and attention. What is inside Rattles body, and how she feels, nobody cares. Nobody knows that inner beauty is influenced by one's personality. Rattles soul is sensual, loving, and generous, willing to offer everything and devote herself. When worried, rattle feels that her brains are buzzing, so she tucks herself into her shell like the shyest snail.

If rattle had its way, it would prefer to hang comfortably around an animal's neck, sensing his warmth and honesty. She believes they can work together to develop trust, emotional connection, and mutual relationships. For the rest of her life, Rattle deserves a nice mate. They may live as Adam and Eve did in heaven. Then all the diverse musical tones might float through the air, celebrating and praising life. Rattle recognizes that the animal, which she decided to wrap his neck around, needed greater respect.

An animal's existence becomes difficult and challenging when it is excluded from paradise without justification. Rattle would spend his entire life with his animal lover as a result of realising this. She understands that an animal's future is harsh and that her fate is cruel, whether it is to live without love, serve only as a milking machine, or ultimately find itself in someone else's stomach. The ornament will bring joy to the lives of the depressed animal since she is selfless. Rattle prefers to amuse the cow throughout the duration of its life.

Cymbals

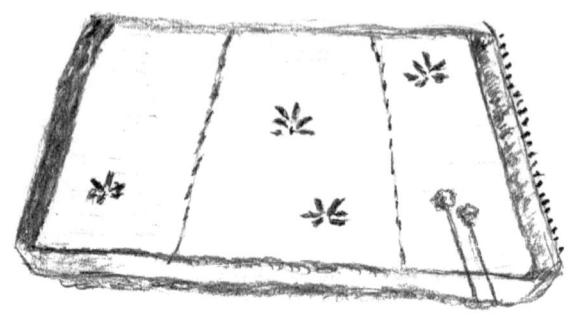

To make the cymbals speak, you'll need two snowball-like wooden balls. As they strike the strings, they give the soul wings and raise the spirit to worship the church's vaults. Shepherd typically picks a whip over a cymbal since it appears to be sweeter, especially one that is suitable for scaring away stupid and noisy insects.

Not too many people know that the perfection in playing cymbals in this world can be achieved by anyone who loves the language of cymbals and who is passionate in learning to play them and ready to devote his life to it. If perfection is attained, even the illiterate can be honoured with God's and community's recognition.

Jankelis, a Lithuanian child of Israel, was named the greatest among the cymbal players. When he was younger, his family recalls him despising the intended family rattle and other common childhood pastimes. He grabbed some dropped and already dirty balls in a corner when he first started crawling, which he found appealing for themselves, and he stuck with those balls for the remainder of his life. They have become an essential part of his life. While others on the corner were seeking to get a taste of a cigar, Jankelis remained committed to his balls, as if a grazing herd was hunting ladies with the goal of settling on her to satisfy unquenchable hormonal hunger and sexual appetite. Jankelis kept his balls when his family pushed him to learn their business techniques. He declined to rule out secrets from his father's business sector, and hid his shillings under the pillow. He also did not sleep with his prospective overweight bride. When Jankelis had more grey hair than the number of strings on the cymbal, his father gave his son's brain the nickname 'silly head'.

The father was furious with his son for exchanging his valuables for some worthless strings that were simply stretched across the table. Jankelis was well aware that he had broken his father's and mother's hearts and deeply buried their hopes. Every day Jankelis fingers were holding wooden balls instead of counting money and figuring out how to keep the money safe. Women stared at the musician all the time, offering almost unreserved love and hugs, but he was blind and deaf to their cheap service. When Jankelis proceeded to the dance floor, instead of dancing, he gazed up into the sky, searching for his place in Heaven. He wished to be blessed and recognised for his abilities there.

Jankelis had no reason to lie, and stuck into women's heads some lies, causing him troubles. He envisioned himself as the best cymbal player in the world. After mastering his musical abilities, the cymbal player intended to take over his father's business. Money wasn't everything to him, obviously. The singing of Nightingale, not a woman, drove him insane, and he admired her for her voice. She was Jankelis's teacher and he could learn songs from her.

Those who learned to smoke, fell in love with a woman, and drank a lot of wine, remained useless. They were envious of Jankelis's success. Jankelis was improving his playing talents every day until his head was discovered resting on the cymbals one morning. His fingers were icily icily icily icily icily icily icily icily icily. With them, he was buried to sleep.

Brass

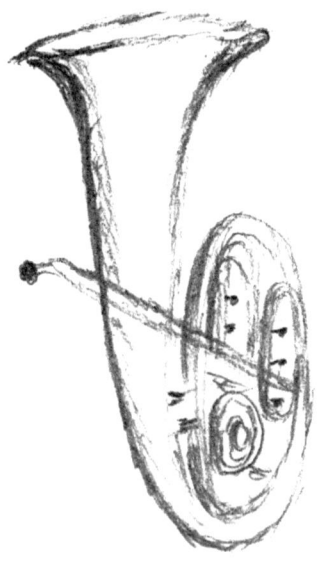

He had been born as an orangutan; the brass was confident. Unfortunately, the exact prehistory of his own success don't remember, including who donated the sperm that allowed him to survive and who conceived and carried him in the womb. His mind was clouded with uncertainty. He was certain he was an ugly orphan who lived in a realm of phantasies and music. Strangers turned their backs on him. When it came time to dance, no one wanted to dance with him since his ungainly, clunky feet weren't very flexible. Worse, when he attempted to communicate with his partner, she flew away as soon as he opened his mouth. His affectionate words were not very pleasant. He was accused because his sentences lacked election, emotion, and sexuality. Love has a certain quality about it. Tube, on the other hand, is certain in his assertion since, unlike a sparrow who squeaks unnecessarily lovingly, he likes to coo like a crow. Tuba and crow go well together. To summarise, everyone has their own musical style and is looking for a unique way to express themselves. Some people will always have the misfortune of putting someone down because they are jealous. Brass, on the other hand, will remain proud and project his nobility to all who encounter him.

Flute

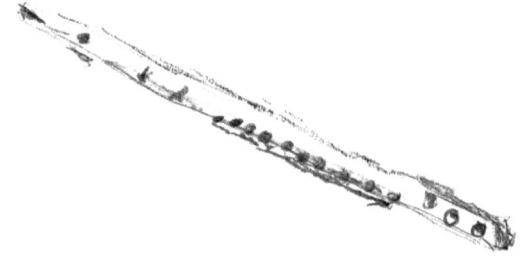

When God changed music into an instrument to express it to mankind, the flute believes she had the form of a bird in a previous existence.

Lips will touch you,' whispered God to her. – As if you were nothing more than a glass of wine –, trying to convince the Flute. After hearing God's words, the flute made the decision to play for joy and rested like a bohemian lady against the player's lips. When the musician, who is also a player, kisses the flute, she flutters in the air and sings like a bird.

Coquette, trombone muttered, enviously glancing at her, who at this point he had developed the look of a log.

He'd happily lie down in her case for the rest of the night, hugging her lovingly. He is extremely passionate about her, and plus muscular, so he would know how to burn flutes wings and win her soul.

Flute is proud of himself and humorous, because had a great history in her past. She recalls that she had a bony appearance a long time ago. Back then, she was created from an animal's rib that was unintentionally given to destroy. It happened when Pharaoh was still alive, and she and him had a terrific time together. The Pharaoh was physically attracted to her outlook. But Flute wasn't fascinated about that because, unfortunately, there was also a foolish comb next to God of Egypt.

Foolish item had no soul residing in her body –, thought Flute loudly –, so there is no way for them to communicate as a human does.

And Flute, as a real bitch showed a lack of respect and courtesy to the Comb as well. The Flute believed egotistically that Comb is overly insensitive and blind to the beauty of the Flute. Only Pharaoh is deserving of respect. Comb meant to brush his hair for this reason, sometimes even twice daily. The interaction gave her life purpose. But Flute persisted in whining, so she continued. Comb belongs to the family of rakes. She kills herself in order to flash her white teeth. Unfortunately, this wretched creation was not endowed with a flawless physique or a dedicated soul. She is gullible and just thinks about temptation.

Aerophone

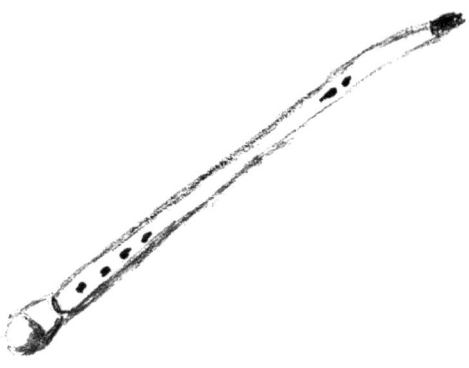

God felt sorry for the cow, who had to suffer so much during her brief life on our planet. And she also was dissatisfied with the way she was treated as an honest animal, and God knew it. The King felt terrible for the cow, because the animal's demeanour was pleasant, akin to that of a hardworking woman, and she was exploited by everyone on each given day and at any given moment.

Whatever happened, the cow's soul remained as serene and serene as a lovely daybreak at a certain time. Despite being attacked by oxen, the animal has never uttered anything unfavourable about anyone. Because of her relentless struggles to survive in the past, God chose her to live in heaven.

The bull was abandoned to suffer from abstinence and live alone for the rest of his life after pursuing her and developing multiple lusts for her. Then God turned his victim, the cow, into an aerophone, which could certainly require horns in the future, and removed bull's horns, making him a helpless and silly-looking creature. The words was said to the cow:

Continued God, "You are free to voice your own truths and mourn over your history.

Since then, the cow has caused the bull to stumble whenever he hears the sweet voice of an old love. He is especially missing the cow's sinless physique and humble spirit.

He regrets that God hasn't seen his best qualities. The bull and cow could coexist for the rest of their days. The bull believed that God had made a mistake by separating them apart.

Since this happened, the former pleasure slave will be separated from his queen and will miss her for days. The previous cow, who has now been turned into an aerophone, sings melodies and expresses gratitude to God for his benevolence and a new life.

Concertina

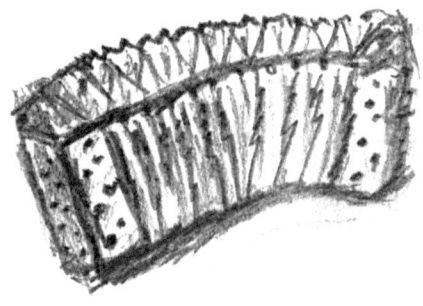

Concertina is aware that she has a large stomach and finds it bothersome that the violin's string suspects her of having weight issues behind her back.

Her figure does not appear to be attractive – the Violin muttered to others, exhibiting Concertina's pain.

Concertina gets irritated when she attempts to compare herself to others. Why does she have such a horrible appearance? She had no idea who had given her this outlook and who the author was. She was fine until someone grabbed her shoulder and started fiddling with her stomach. This act made her realise that she wasn't being treated with respect. But after that, she also learned how to act properly. Now she hides her tummy when no one wants her to be loud. Tummy is her power, but silence is a positive omen. The silence is concealing the truth. It indicates that no one is interested in the lie. When song is needed to kill the silence, however, the tummy swells as unwelcome air enters into Concertina's guts. The melody then gains wings and soars. Concertina adores music and the person who creates it. She sobs when no one notices, because she is missing a truthful partner.

Trumpet

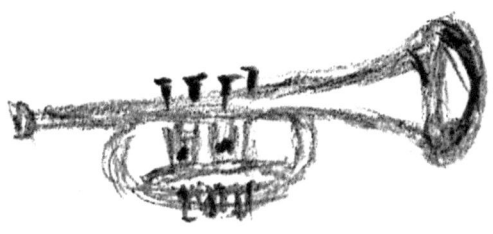

The trumpet was constructed from a rooster's rib, which was chosen to preserve its music. One thing, the rib was difficult to control because the owner, who is a rooster, inherited his father's rebellious personality and behavioural pattern. So everyone had to simmer it in the pot while the rooster's heart melted and his ribs became flexible enough to bend in any direction. The rooster was once known as a fighter, as well as a soldier capable of winning wars, who routinely enticed crows and other foolish birds to brutal combat in order to demonstrate his own might. Once upon a time, God ate his dinner and then glanced down through a cloud. He saw a rooster and the rooster saw him. Their gazes were glued on each other. Because of the rooster's unfriendly appearance, the food stuck in God's mouth. The King of the Universe observed that the rooster who fought everyone was wasting his time and was useless, but he admired him for his voice inexhaustibly. As a result, the choice to make an instrument out of a rooster's rib was made. The bird was in desperate need of his blessings and a soul. The musicality of the rooster's rib has not been lost after its transformation into an instrument. He sends his tunes into space to fly, overcoming even birds.

Tabla Drum

The drum has no hands, no face, no lips, no ears and is nevertheless considered ugly creature. No private life seen by an unfriendly eye. For those people who are unable to immerse themselves in the world of sounds and do not hear them the truth is their ears are insensitive. That's why they are unable to distinguish when the drum forwards his message to the world and humanity. In the real world, the drum's language is simple and accurate, with no lies or inaccuracies of course.

When someone fool knocks him, he does not complain because he was born in a straightforward manner that originated from a stump. The same fate befalls his father and grandmother who are resting now in peace.

Chordophone

The development of the chordophone took more than several years. It was indicated by passion. In the dark night, a formerly elderly guy thought it was his own woman's body and brushed his chilly hand across the table. The thought of discovering desire in her caused him to become a little drunk and oblivious. The man came close to grasping her by the waist while still wearing his pants. He couldn't have been satisfied because his pants were still on. Went to bed and cuddled up to himself instead of continuing to search for a warmer body that may cause him to shout like a wild stream. The following day, he decided to embrace the Spruce tree and fashion a lady to suit his needs. He was getting ready up until the day when a string accidently appeared on the wooden body. He centred his wants in this manner. He imagined the appearance of the instrument. He can develop his life music, he thought. Strings are like arteries. Strings on this table are more than the soul can reflect thoughts. Dark and light tones fit into his created instrument. Unfortunately, the melody which comes out of the instrument without words looks sad because the Spruce tree does not smile. The wood does not respond like a woman would. The wood's body is cold, just arteries trying to talk to him when he touches it. You can talk, but nothing in return, just produces sound sometimes lighter than sunset. So, what has the man accomplished? Just tightness in the man's throat and in his heart which is slightly relieved when he attempts to transfer it to his instrument. Music was designed by him to take the burden off the heart.

Taiko drum

The stump was once a hard-hearted guy. Because of his continual lack of self, he turned into wood. Being a stump gave him time to consider his options and come to the best conclusion for himself, so he wasn't dissatisfied by it. Reincarnation was intended to benefit him in some way.

He did not, however, possess a passport bearing his mother's name. He didn't know what he wanted to do when he grew up and became a man, or what his future would be like in ten years. No thought was given to the future; just the body was fed in order for the muscles to develop.

The image of His Mother persisted even after she became unbreathable.

He muttered, 'She was the most caring person I've ever encountered.' Even the sun or the rain couldn't be as kind to him as she was. She was also her favourite creation.

He always had a stump-like countenance that only communicated power and aggression. Nothing pertaining to the advancement of humanity or more uplifting concepts went unnoticed. He also rejected the idea of God's grace, though. No matter what, God always made an effort to make things better for him by giving him options, but his existence was too short for any lasting changes. When the tree on its grave has died and dried up, it has been transformed into a true stump.

EIN HERZ FÜR AUTOREN A HEART FOR AUTHORS À L'ÉCOUTE DES AUTEURS MIA K
HJÄRTA FÖR FÖRFATTARE UN CORAZÓN POR LOS AUTORES YAZARLARIMIZA GÖN
CUORE PER AUTORI ET HJERTE FOR FORFATTERE EEN HART VOOR SCHRIJVERS T
ERZŐINKÉRT SERCE DLA AUTORÓW EIN HERZ FÜR AUTOREN A HEART FOR AUT
ORAÇÃO ВСЕЙ ДУШОЙ К АВТОРАМ ETT HJÄRTA FÖR FÖRFATTARE À LA ESCUCHA
AUTEURS MIA ΚΑΡΔΙΑ ΓΙΑ ΣΥΓΓΡΑΦΕΙΣ UN CUORE PER AUTORI ET HJERTE FOR FOR
YAZARLARIMI ERZŐINKÉRT SERCE DLA AUTORÓW

The author

Nijolė Kavaliauskaitė – Hunter is a former artist who was born in Lithuania. She spent a lot of time on the keyboard. After many hours alone with an instrument, she began to feel that it was her best buddy. Being a music educator, she dedicated her life to teaching kids music's language. She has previously written stories to help children see and find relationships between music and their surroundings.